名流詩叢 51

太陽之子
The Son of Sun

李魁賢 台華英三語詩集

排灣族老司機
臉上皺紋像花東縱谷
北大武山嶽峰連綿
有五位兒女七位孫子
太陽永遠不會休息

李魁賢 (Lee Kuei-shien) ◎ 著

前言
Foreword

　　虛歲88，寫詩超過70年，半上路下，可是詩變成生活的大部分，敢若是生命的主要成分，規日迷佇詩內底，除詩以外，無所求，無啥事誌通好做。詩所關懷，無形中傾向大自然，心靈佮自然和諧，就會清心、靜心、寬心。到老來承蒙秀威支持，完成替詩貢獻少寡力量的真濟大願望，心肝內感戴不盡，啥物話嘛講袂了。

　　虛歲88，寫詩逾70年，所學無成，惟詩成為生活的大部分，彷彿是生命的主要成分，整天沉緬詩中，除詩外，無所求，無所事事。詩所關懷，無形中傾向自然，心靈與自然合拍，即清心、靜心、寬心。晚年承蒙秀威支持，完成為詩貢獻微力的許多大願，衷心感戴，夫復何言。

As an old man being 88 years of nominal age and having been writing poetry for more than 70 years, I have achieved nothing in my studies, but as a matter of fact, poetry has become the major part of my living, and as if it is the main component of my life. I am obsessed with poetry all day long, apart from poetry, I have nothing to ask for and nothing to do. What concerned by my poems are invisibly inclined to the great nature, and my soul is in tune with great nature, that is, pure, calm and relaxed. In my later years, I deeply thank to Showwe's support for help me to accomplish many of great wishes to make my subtle contribution to poetry. I am so sincerely grateful that no more to say.

目次

前言 Foreword　003

| 台語篇

太陽之子　014

百步之鄉　016

基隆登高　017

路思義教堂　019

百年秀喜──紀念詩人陳秀喜百歲　020

四草綠色磅空　022

隔離　023

淡水文化園區　024

鼠麴粿　026

銅像笑容　027

數念忠寮　028

淡水音樂會　029

烏克蘭日頭花　030

落葉　031

我的書　032

河景　034

望高樓　035

佇金鬱金香夢地　036

忠寮詩路　037

白翎鷥雕塑　038

捏瓷仔　039

設想　040

下凡　041

回想淡水古早初次落雪　042

捐書——予淡江大學覺生紀念圖書館　043

和平公園　044

我的詩句　045

詩修養人生──予詩人李昌憲　046

歌聲對肯亞帶來　047

毒蠍　049

笠作稿一甲子　050

予台南的情詩　051

| 華語篇

太陽之子　054

百步之鄉　056

基隆登高　057

路思義教堂　059

百年秀喜──紀念詩人陳秀喜百年　060

四草綠色隧道　062

隔離　063

淡水文化園區　064

鼠麴粿　066

銅像笑容　067

想念忠寮　068

淡水音樂會　069

烏克蘭向日葵　070

落葉　071

我的書　072

河景　074

望高樓　075

在金鬱金香夢土上　076

忠寮詩路　077

白鷺鷥塑像　078

製陶　079

想像　080

下凡　081

憶淡水早年初雪　082

捐書──給淡江大學覺生紀念圖書館　083

和平公園　084

我的詩句　085

詩陶冶人生──給詩人李昌憲　086

歌聲來自肯亞　087

毒蠍　088

笠農一甲子　089

給台南的情詩　090

| 英語篇

The Son of Sun   092

Hometown of the Hundred-Pacer Vipers   094

Climbing up the Hilltop in Keelung   095

The Luce Chapel   097

Centennial Elegance and Happiness   098

Green Tunnel at Sicao   100

Isolation   101

Tamsui Arts & Cultural Park   102

Cudweed Herbal Rice Cakes   104

Bronze Statue Smile   105

Longing for Tiong-liâu   106

Tamsui Concert   107

Sunflower in Ukraine   108

Fallen Leaves   109

My Books   110

River View   112

Sky Hall   113

On Dreamland of Golden Tulip   114

Tiong-liâu Poetry Road   115

The Statues of Egrets   116

Making Pottery   117

Imagination   118

Descending to the Human World   119

In Memory of First Snow in Early Year at Tamsui   120

Book Donation ——To Chueh-sheng Memorial Library of Tamkang University   121

The Peace Park   122

My Verses　　123

Poetry Cultivates Our Life
——To poet Lee Chang-hsien　　124

The Songs come from Kenya　　126

Poisonous Scorpions　　128

As a "Li" Poetry Farmer for 60 Years　　129

A Love Poem to Tainan　　130

著者簡介 About Poet　　131

台語篇

排灣族的老司機
面肉皺紋如像花東縱谷
北大武山峰峰相連
有五個子女七個孫
日頭永遠免休睏

太陽之子

對金峰去達仁鄉的路兮
太陽之子
皮膚烏烏的老司機
對我講：
「阮台東的火車
無燒土炭無吃電
是啉小米酒兮！」
莫怪真勇真猛向前衝
腳輪仔少寡無穩
搖搖晃晃
排灣族的老司機
面肉皺紋如像花東縱谷
北大武山峰峰相連
有五個子女七個孫
日頭永遠免休睏
對外面來到遮

無張持予海湧沖到沙埔
無人抾的海螺仔殼
單獨佇聽海湧聲

2020.07.18

百步之鄉

神聖日頭光

對金黃色山頂

透早射落來路面頂

我對金崙行向賓茂村

家家有百步蛇圖騰守護

有寡青翠山崙做後門屏風

百步之內四界有小米、佾洛神花

紅藜、咖啡、釋迦，毋是擺好看

我食過一世人上芳純品種

沿金崙溪半焦燥半湍流

庄跤人紛紛迎接日光

無閒農業生產工課

遊覽車未發動

等人浸礦水

2020.07.19

基隆登高

佇基隆容軒步道
透早踏就石級仔
期待復較懸一層的風景
真濟鬍鬚拖落土的
大榕樹密集集的樹葉菴蓋內底
鳥仔群合唱曲開始交響樂
雜草野花沿路對我揢手
舉頭看白雲微微仔笑
經過風雨的洗禮
佇內心轉變成詩意
石級仔彎彎斡斡
總是一路引導我向懸行
到嶺頂觀景平台
看出去闊莽莽的海洋
展現走傱的氣魄
用海湧捙跋反對付遠洋挑戰

恬恬獨立佇嶺頂
感受台灣島嶼祖國
孤守佇天地之間無漏氣

2020.09.30

路思義教堂

透早
鐘
佇安靜睏眠中
傳來清悠的聲音
引導我來到遮
佇鐘樓頭前越頭
看著你舉雙手合掌
向天頂祈禱
雲透露出
一絲仔早起時日頭光
照射佇
你的指頭仔尾
我真想欲倒佇周圍的
青翠土地
做永久的眠床

2020.11.15

百年秀喜
——紀念詩人陳秀喜百歲

瑛瑛將妳留落來的

淺茄色玉仔

掛佇我胸坎前

妳的形影

即刻出現佇我心肝頂

玉仔正面

雕刻鯉魚跳龍門

我一直守佇詩的籠仔門

玉仔後面

雕刻花開富貴

我努力追求美的回歸

紀念詩人秀喜百歲

這塊玉仔遂變成

我得到賜福的

秀喜標誌

＊2020年抵好是笠詩社前社長陳秀喜女士百歲生日，11月14日笠
年會時，承蒙陳社長千金瑛瑛贈送社長在生上愛的淺茄色玉仔
一塊，到旦逐日掛在我胸坎前，表示誠意懷念。

2020.11.17

四草綠色磅空

古早經過黑色磅空

土炭粉滿天飛

四箍輪轉烏烏暗暗

忽然間一逝強烈白光

予人神魂四散

今也褸過綠色磅空

竹排仔勻勻也划過

周圍誠葱的紅樹林

變成青翠河流

對葉仔縫射落來的日頭光

佇水中反射出另外一片世界

有紅螯師舉螯準旗仔撲

佇夢中相拚仙

2021.03.24

隔離

我佮社會隔離
單獨守書房
疫情流行的緣故

規群鳥仔隔離鳥仔籠
倒轉去樹林
佇樹欉中間自由飛

心佮身隔離
進行國際詩交流
無受阻礙

咱的國土
佮歹厝邊隔離
變成獨立實體

2021.06.08

淡水文化園區

以前我聽過
輕便火車噗噗喘的聲音
幫浦抽送臭油的齊勻聲音
製罐工場摃白鐵仔的機械聲音
水上飛行機佇河面起落的噴水聲音
美軍飛行機揮炸彈火燒臭油棧的爆炸聲音

然後變成
磚仔瓦佇落雨天哼哼叫的聲音
草仔枝佇日頭跤歡喜笑的聲音
熱天蟬仔熱烈呼喚生命的聲音
蝶仔清悠拍翼招蜂迢迢的聲音
大樹孤單抵風反抗壓迫的聲音

今也常常聽著
社區大學上課的智慧聲音
新書發表會念詩的溫柔聲音
音樂會少年郎反應的激情聲音
書畫展參觀者內心的欣賞聲音
各地遊客懷舊探新的笑談聲音

2021.08.13

鼠麴粿

詩人

來到忠寮石牆仔內

大家用寫詩的手

來做鼠麴粿

無論紅豆仔粿

抑是菜脯粿

或者芋仔粿

蒸熟了後

餡每一絲絲

統是詩

2021.09.20

銅像笑容

銅像引起爭論
敢會使霸占遐爾懸空間
毋管有人結群去抗議
佇廣場喊激烈口號
銅像自頭到尾出現笑容
彼是無實在的本性
鑄造冷卻後定型變成
惡質的冷笑
在生酷刑屠殺百姓
滿足信徒製造來服侍
毋管安怎爭論
留佇歷史上
予人冷笑

2020.10.03

數念忠寮

忠寮山水是天賜的
忠寮田園是祖先開墾的
忠寮文化是世代努力的
我少年時蹛佇忠寮
我中年時離開忠寮
我食老倒轉來忠寮
一世人經過詩洗禮了後
我迭迭數念忠寮
愛的最後基地
安息所在

2021.10.05

淡水音樂會

佇淡水河邊
杜聰明傑出的詩
譜成曲的旋律佇飄揚
我予秋風迷去
恰如展翼的淡水鷗鴞
佇巴拉卡*
大片岩壁頭前飛起飛落
啊，我的少年夢
還復是佇飄浪摸無路
佇秋風聲聲呼喚中
猶未醒起來

＊杜聰明博士故居佇巴拉卡深山裡，對忠寮會當看著巴拉卡大片
　岩壁。

2021.10.16

烏克蘭日頭花

注日頭花種子
囥入去軍衣橐袋仔內
準備佇戰場用肉身
化成土做培養基
用紅血灌溉
佇烏克蘭主權國土

記心記肝新婦交代
該由新製的軍衣見證
復員後共同來栽培
保護國花品種
向天頂微微仔笑
佇烏克蘭自由國土

2022.02.27

落葉

規排
雨傘樹
一夜之間
黃葉落到規塗跤
對遠遠
突然間傳來
飛彈轟炸的影像
生命佮落葉共款
倒規塗跤
予人掃去溝仔底
輕採掩掩埋埋兮

2022.03.08

我的書

我的書
是一世人對故鄉永遠的
懷念

我的書
是朋友予我一點一滴累積的
營養

我的書
是由外國遠洋過海來寄恬的
思想

我的書
是台灣重重疊疊脫離袂掉的
情愛

我的書
是淡水故鄉予我最後的
疼惜

2022.07.26

河景

一滴水,二滴水,三滴水……
流入邊仔的圳溝
復育變成魚蝦休閒園區
匯聚河川水流
經過長途拚勢
來到心情平靜的淡水河
順遂將日頭揀到河口
歷史的回音變渺小
烏暗中還復少寡聽有
觀音山跤光明燈光起來矣
一隻小隻船仔佇河面勻勻也移動
親像佇換鏈仔
欲予河水目珠瞌瞌休睏

2022.09.18

望高樓

爬高看遠

看透歷史長河

人生喜樂

拚勢四界觀望

宛然英雄

再世講淡水故事

講到爽

世間烏幕放落來

燈光起來

就欲轉移陣地

準備另外一場奮鬥

2022.09.18

佇金鬱金香夢地

透早日頭光由東爿來

觀音山頂

干單賰少寡白頭毛雲絲

鳥隻並我較早起來

佇我窗仔口

飛來飛去探看

世間安靜到

我甘願留佇夢地

佇金鬱金香的胸坎

無想欲精神

2022.09.18

忠寮詩路

每一條路統通到茨
每一工出門統是行轉去茨的路
佇我永遠的故鄉
借問忠寮詩路通到佗位
順圳溝水清悠悠
陪鳥仔聲吱吱叫
復有竹葉綴風沙沙
有時還復有姑婆芋的大掌
掠著無細膩落落來的雨滴嘻嘻嘩嘩
斟酌聽詩對你輕聲細說
佇忠寮詩路
一步一步行向心靈的茨

2022.09.19

白翎鷥雕塑

大屯山跤
白翎鷥巡田水
復有水牛、稻田
組合成農村耕作畫面
是我少年時的記持
安詳、和樂
到今七十年過去囉
農地轉型
變成活趒的生態園區
白翎鷥遷徙陣地
固定倚佇桂花樹跤
指引詩路方向

2022.09.22

捏瓷仔

來喔！
用妳溫柔的手
共我拍、共我搵、共我搥
共我苔到扁扁的身材
猶原堅持充分抵抗素質
共我用模仔成型
共我捏成器材
共我油漆溫暖素色
復加一粒啟明星
永遠指引
獨立前進的方向

2022.10.04

設想

佇彎曲的茨頂
起落無平的草埔
種兩位鬱金香
一位集合成番薯島型
另外一位迤成心型
每工金色日頭光
親像東方博士
前來朝聖
總是會記得
向露水講出心聲：
我愛台灣！

2022.10.08

下凡

夢見穿著黑色細腰闊裾
洋裝的女畫家
出現佇山崙頂懸懸的教堂門前
身材較贏級仔的彎幹
頭鬃螺仔頂插一蕊黃花
並街仔路樹頂的生花復較生
Buenos días, señor!
Buenos días, señorita!
美俗詩佇無言中競爭
創作佇神聖時刻完成
注心靈對懸級仔
送往下凡的世間
佇我恍神的時瞬
雞啼囉

2022.12.05

回想淡水古早初次落雪

紛紛飛落落來的雪

不停佇思念

頂世人毋會袂記得的情

到這世人無法度絕念的緣分

雪紛紛飛落落來的時瞬

世間一片白茫茫

彼種寒冷

變成心中不由自主的溫暖

留落來無限鄉愁

雪真難忘

2023.08.28

捐書
——予淡江大學覺生紀念圖書館

我書房的藏書
是一世人毋變的數念
累積我毋知會變啥款的夢想
毋甘嫌毋甘放捒的承諾
移交予故鄉的淡江大學圖書館
佔領五虎崗的一個山頭
傳播永世相續的歷史芳味
總是會拄著有緣的人
鼻著藏書中的祕傳
心靈相拄的一霎仔久
種籽落土
自然舉頭看大屯山日出
養育台灣的鄉愁

2022.09.02

和平公園

遠遠看淡海
延伸台灣海峽
海天無限迴國際
舉頭看觀音山
靜心養性
遠遠遠迴到極樂世界
佇和平公園
滬尾藝文步道
詩畫創作表現的景觀
佮大自然同齊
有一欉虛擬菩提樹
永遠栽佇心肝內

2023.09.17

我的詩句

我的詩句
是自由孤獨的字詞
自然天成的排列
失誤走入去圖書館書林
茫茫渺渺失去方向
自由留佇無話的空間
變成孤獨的詩
孤孤單單
敢若我黃昏的形影

2023.09.22

詩修養人生
——予詩人李昌憲

你佇浪漫的青春歲月

開始寫關懷現實的詩

你佇電子工廠從事管理工作

思思念念的是女工的生活

你佇中年出國推動國際合作

前後勿會袂記得台灣的安全

你佇食頭路退休的年歲

體驗苦澀帶甘的茶藝人生

你佇寫詩有成就以外

復從事書法、印刻佮捏瓷仔

今也我看著你的藝術創作

注詩句燒製茶杯仔

予人人將詩情飲落去

詩媦永遠留佇世間

2023.09.24

歌聲對肯亞帶來

歌聲對肯亞帶來
音樂家翁必洛用家己做的八弦牛皮音鼓
配合大聲嚨喉的歌聲
親像欲將聽眾的神魂摸去
對山崙頂學府音樂廳
到飯店望高樓
到忠寮社區
到遠望淡水河的螺仔殼廳
佇連續不斷的尾聲
最後是伊臨時為我譜的曲
予我心頭醉茫茫
十支指頭亂舞

＊肯亞音樂家翁必洛（Wilfred Ombiro）陪肯亞詩人克里斯多
福・歐肯姆瓦（Christopher Okemwa）出席2023年淡水福爾摩
莎國際詩歌節，伊拍鼓演唱真受歡迎，閉幕晚會時，演奏臨時
為我譜的曲，充滿熱情。

2023.09.30

毒蠍

毒蠍是恐怖份子
舉懸長螯
看著對風微微也笑的花蕊
就拆破花瓣共伊皆掇
拄著認真勞動的狗蟻
就屠殺無辜
中東天頂紛紛落落來的
不是同情的目水
是復較毒復較狠的火箭飛彈
揚起來的煙火
無法度掩蓋心靈

＊2023年10月7日，巴勒斯坦激進組織哈瑪斯無張持發射數千
　粒火箭飛彈，轟炸以色列，引起中東以哈戰爭。皆掇（Che`
　tuah）意思是用暴力對付。

2023.10.13

笠作穡一甲子

遇到妳

從此一世人作穡

戴笠仔

努力耕作詩的田園

佇都市高樓樹林內奔波

走揣生活營養素質

佇字詞深層的礦區挖掘

篩檢頭前的人拍交落的寶藏

佇思想的奧祕山脈巡迴

探索發見新領土

堅守六十冬

漸漸消瘦落肉

恰如焦柴頭

2023.10.15

予台南的情詩

拍莓辛苦四百冬
期待開花時燦揚揚的笑容
吸引眾人共同欣賞
對雲層透露出來的月光

2023.11.24

華語篇

排灣族老司機
臉上皺紋像花東縱谷
北大武山嶽峰連綿
有五位兒女七位孫子
太陽永遠不會休息

太陽之子

從金峰往達仁鄉路上
太陽之子
銅色皮膚的老司機
對我說：
「我們台東的火車
不燒煤不吃電
是喝小米酒的！」
難怪勇猛向前衝
腳輪有點不穩
搖搖顛顛
排灣族老司機
臉上皺紋像花東縱谷
北大武山嶽峰連綿
有五位兒女七位孫子
太陽永遠不會休息
外來此地

意外被海浪沖到沙灘上
無人撿拾的貝殼
獨自聽潮音

2020.07.18

百步之鄉

神聖陽光

從金黃色山峰

撒鋪在清晨道路上

我從金崙走往賓茂村

家家有百步蛇圖騰守護

有些翠綠山岡做後門屏風

百步之內處處有小米，和洛神花

紅藜、咖啡、釋迦，不是供觀賞

我遍嘗平生難得香純品種

沿金崙溪半乾涸半暢流

鄉民已紛紛迎著陽光

忙著農業生產工作

遊覽車還不動

等人泡湯

2020.07.19

基隆登高

在基隆容軒步道
清晨踏上石階
期待更上一層的風景
眾多鬍鬚垂地的
大榕樹葉叢內
群鳥合唱曲開始交響
雜草野花沿途向我招手
抬頭看到白雲在微笑
經過風風雨雨的洗禮
在心靈裡化成詩意
石階曲曲折折
總是一路引導我向上
直到嶺頂觀景平台
眺望壯闊的海洋
展現奔騰的氣魄
洶湧海流對付遠方挑戰

默默獨立在嶺頂
感受台灣島嶼祖國
無愧孤守在天地之間

2020.09.30

路思義教堂

清晨
鐘
安靜睡眠中
有悠悠的聲音
引導我來到此地
在鐘樓前回首
看到你雙手合掌
朝向天上祈禱
雲間透露
一抹初旭
照耀在
你的指尖
我好想躺在周圍的
青翠大地
做為永久的眠床

2020.11.15

百年秀喜
——紀念詩人陳秀喜百年

瑛瑛把妳遺留的

淡紫玉珮

掛在我胸前

妳的形影

立刻呈現在我心上

玉珮正面

雕刻鯉躍龍門

我一直廝守詩的籠門

玉珮背面

雕刻花開富貴

我努力追求美的復歸

紀念詩人秀喜百年

這玉珮成為

我獲得賜福的

秀喜標誌

＊2020年適逢笠詩社前社長陳秀喜女士百年冥誕，11月14日笠年
　會時，承陳社長千金瑛瑛贈送社長生前喜愛的淡紫色玉珮一
　枚，迄今天天掛在我胸前，誠致懷念。

2020.11.17

四草綠色隧道

以前經過黑色隧道

煤塵瀰漫空間

周圍黑暗

猛然一道強烈白光

令人神魂四散

如今通過綠色隧道

竹筏緩緩滑過

周圍盎然紅樹林

構成碧綠河道

葉隙間投下日光

水中倒影另一片世界

有招潮蟹舉螯當旗招搖

在夢裡輝映

2021.03.24

隔離

我與社會隔離
獨守書房
疫情流行的緣故

群鳥隔離鳥籠
回到林中
在樹間自由飛翔

心與身隔離
進行國際詩交流
不受阻礙

我們國土
與惡鄰隔離
成為獨立實體

2021.06.08

淡水文化園區

以前我聽到
輕便火車的喘息聲音
幫浦抽送臭油的順暢聲音
製罐敲打白鐵的機械聲音
水上飛機河面起降的噴濺聲音
美機炸彈火燒油棧的驚慌聲音

然後變成
磚瓦在雨中呻吟的聲音
小草在陽光下歡笑的聲音
夏蟬熱烈呼喚生命的聲音
蝴蝶悠然拍翼招蜂遨遊的聲音
大樹孤獨臨風抗拒壓制的聲音

如今常聽到
社區大學上課的智慧聲音
新書發表會念詩的溫柔聲音
音樂會年輕亢奮的激情聲音
書畫展參觀者內心的讚賞聲音
各地訪客懷舊探新的談笑聲音

2021.08.13

鼠麴粿

詩人

來到忠寮石牆子內

大家用寫詩的手

製作鼠麴粿

無論是紅豆粿

或是蘿蔔乾粿

還是芋頭粿

蒸熟後

內餡每一絲絲

都是詩

2021.09.20

銅像笑容

銅像引起爭論
該不該霸占那高聳空間
不管有人成群去抗議
在廣場喊激烈口號
銅像始終露出笑容
那是不真實本性
鑄造冷卻後定型成
嚴酷的冷笑
生前肆虐屠殺人民
滿足於信徒製造歌頌
不管怎麼爭論
留在歷史上
讓人冷笑

2020.10.03

想念忠寮

忠寮山水是天賜的
忠寮田園是祖先開墾的
忠寮文化是世代努力的
我的少年住在忠寮
我的中年疏遠忠寮
我的老年回歸忠寮
一生經過詩的洗禮後
我常常想念忠寮
愛的最後基地
安息所在

2021.10.05

淡水音樂會

在淡水河畔
杜聰明傑出的詩
譜成曲的旋律在飄揚
我沉醉在秋風裡
彷彿振翼的淡水老鷹
在巴拉卡＊
巨大岩壁前飄舉
啊，我的少年夢
依然飄蕩不著邊際
在秋風聲聲呼喚中
猶未醒來

＊杜聰明博士故居在巴拉卡深山裡，從忠寮可以遙望巴拉卡一
　大塊岩壁。

2021.10.16

烏克蘭向日葵

把向日葵種子
放入征衣口袋裡
準備在戰場以肉身
化為塵土培養基
以鮮血灌溉
在烏克蘭主權國土上

牢記新婦叮嚀
要以新縫征衣見證
復員共同栽植
保護國花的品種
朝天空微笑
在烏克蘭自由國土上

2022.02.27

落葉

整排

小葉欖仁

一夜間

黃葉掉落滿地

遠方

突然傳來

飛彈轟炸的視訊

生命和黃葉一樣

橫陳大地

掃到壕溝內

草草掩埋

2022.03.08

我的書

我的書
是一生對故鄉永遠的
懷念

我的書
是朋友給我點滴累積的
營養

我的書
是從異邦飄洋渡海寄寓的
思想

我的書
是台灣層層脫離不掉的
情愛

我的書
是淡水故鄉給我最後的
疼惜

2022.07.26

河景

一滴水，二滴水，三滴水……
流入旁側小溪
復育成魚蝦休閒園區
匯聚川流
經長途跋涉
到達心情平靜的淡水河
順勢把夕陽推到河口
歷史的迴聲已渺
黑暗中尚依稀可聞
觀音腳下亮起光明燈
一葉小舟在河上緩緩移動
好像拉動拉鏈
要讓河水閉目休息

2022.09.18

望高樓

登高望遠

望盡歷史長河

人生喜樂

極目馳騁左右

儼然英雄

再世講談淡水故事

等盡興

黑幕落下

燈亮起

就要轉移陣地

準備另一場奮鬥

2022.09.18

在金鬱金香夢土上

旭日從東方來

觀音山頂

只剩白髮雲絲少許

鳥比我早起

在我窗口

飛來飛去探望

人間安靜到

但願留在夢土上

在金鬱金香的懷抱裡

不想醒來

2022.09.18

忠寮詩路

　　條條道路通往家
　　天天出門走回家的路
　　在我永恆的故鄉
　　借問忠寮詩路通往何處
　　順小溪水幽幽
　　伴鳥鳴吱吱喳喳
　　夾雜竹葉隨風沙沙響
　　有時還有姑婆芋的巨掌
　　抓住不小心掉下的雨滴嬉鬧
　　聆聽詩對你輕聲低語
　　在忠寮詩路
　　一步一步走往心靈的家

2022.09.19

白鷺鷥塑像

大屯山麓
白鷺鷥巡田水
加上水牛、稻田
組合成鄉村農耕畫面
是我少年時的記憶
安詳、和樂
如今七十年過去啦
農地轉型
成為活躍生態園區
白鷺鷥遷移陣地
固定站在桂花樹下
指引詩路方向

2022.09.22

製陶

來吧！
用妳溫柔的手
拍我、揉我、擀我
把我壓成扁平的身材
仍然堅持充分抵抗素質
把我模塑成型
捏我成器
把我彩飾溫馨素色
加上一顆啟明星
永遠指引
獨立行進的方向

2022.10.04

想像

在曲面屋頂
波浪形草坪滑坡上
種植兩處鬱金香
一處集成番薯島型
另一處繞成心型
每天金色陽光
像東方博士
前來朝聖
不忘
向露珠傾訴：
我愛台灣！

2022.10.08

下凡

夢見穿著黑色細腰寬襬
洋裝的女畫家
出現在山崗上高聳教堂門前
身段勝似階梯的曲折
髮髻插一朵黃花
比街道樹上鮮花還要鮮豔
Buenos días, señor!
Buenos días, señorita!
美與詩在無言中競爭
創作在神聖時刻完成
把心靈從高階
送往下凡的人間
在我恍神的時刻
雞啼啦

2022.12.05

憶淡水早年初雪

紛紛飄落的雪
不斷的思念
從前世不能遺忘的情
到今生無法絕念的緣分
雪紛紛飄落時
世間空茫茫一片
那種寒冷
化成心中不由自己的溫暖
留下無限鄉愁
雪真難忘

2023.08.28

捐書
——給淡江大學覺生紀念圖書館

我書房的藏書
是一生不渝的眷念
蘊蓄我不知所終的夢想
不離不棄的承諾
移交給故鄉的淡江大學圖書館
據有五虎崗的一個山頭
傳播永世相續的歷史芳香
總會遇到有緣人
聞到藏書中的祕傳
靈犀相觸的剎那
種子落地
自然仰望大屯山日出
孕育台灣的鄉愁

2022.09.02

和平公園

眺望淡海

延伸台灣海峽

海闊天空通往國際

仰望觀音山

靜心養性

遠遠遠達極樂世界

在和平公園

滬尾藝文步道

詩畫創作呈現的景觀

與大自然同在

有一棵虛擬菩提樹

永遠植立心中

2023.09.17

我的詩句

我的詩句
是自由孤獨的字詞
自由天成的排列
誤入圖書館書林
茫然失去方向
自由留存無言的空間
成為孤獨的詩
孤孤單單
如我入暮的身影

2023.09.22

詩陶冶人生
——給詩人李昌憲

你在浪漫的青春歲月
開始寫關懷現實的詩
你在電子工廠從事管理工作
時時念念的是女工的生活
你在中年出國推動國際合作
始終忘懷不掉台灣的安全
你在職場退休的年歲
體驗苦澀帶甘的茶藝人生
你在寫詩有成的餘裕
投身書法、印刻和陶藝
現在我看到你的藝術創作
把詩句燒成茶杯
讓我們把詩情喝下去
詩美永遠留存世間

2023.09.24

歌聲來自肯亞

歌聲來自肯亞
音樂家翁必洛以自製八弦牛皮音鼓
配合激昂歌聲
好像要把聽眾的神魂攝走
從崗上學府音樂廳
到飯店望高樓
到忠寮社區
到眺望淡水河的貝殼廳
在縈迴不斷的餘音裡
最後他譜給我的即興曲
讓我心靈沉醉
十指飛舞

＊肯亞音樂家翁必洛（Wilfred Ombiro）陪伴肯亞詩人克里斯多
　福‧歐肯姆瓦（Christopher Okemwa）出席2023淡水福爾摩莎
　國際詩歌節，演唱大受歡迎，閉幕晚宴時，蒙譜曲賞賜。

2023.09.30

毒蠍

毒蠍舉起長螯
看到迎風微笑的花朵
就撕瓣摧殘
遇見勤於勞動的螞蟻
就屠殺無辜
中東天空紛紛落下的
不是同情的淚水
是更為毒辣的火箭彈
揚起的火焰黑煙
無法蒙蔽心靈

＊2023年10月7日巴勒斯坦激進組織哈瑪斯（Hamas）發射數千枚
　火箭彈，偷襲以色列，引起激烈以哈戰爭。

2023.10.13

笠農一甲子

遇到妳

從此終生務農

戴著笠

致力耕耘詩田園

在都市高樓叢林間奔波

尋求生活營養質素

在字詞深層的礦區挖掘

篩檢前人遺落的寶藏

在思想的奧祕山脈巡迴

探索發現新領地

堅守六十年

逐漸逐漸憔悴

形如槁木

2023.10.15

給台南的情詩

四百年含苞辛苦
期待燦爛花期的笑容
吸引眾人共賞
從雲層露出的月光

2023.11.24

英語篇

The old driver belongs Paiwan tribe
with wrinkles on the face like East Rift Valley
and Meli-miligang Mountains extensive continuously,
he has five children and seven grandchildren
because the sun never rests.

The Son of Sun

On the road from Jinfeng toward Daren township,

the old driver, the son of sun,

with copper colored skin,

says to me:

"The train in our Taitung is

neither burning coals nor eating electricity

but drinking millet wine! "

No wonder it runs forward bravely

and the wheels are a little bit unstable

in rocking.

The old driver belongs Paiwan tribe

with wrinkles on the face like East Rift Valley

and Meli-miligang Mountains extensive continuously,

he has five children and seven grandchildren

because the sun never rests.

As the outsider, a sea shell is unexpectedly

rushed onto the beach by the waves,

no one to pick it up,

and let it be alone in listening the tide sounds.

2020.07.18

Hometown
of the Hundred-Pacer Vipers

Holy sunshine

emerges from the golden peak

paving over roads in the early morning.

I walk from Kanadun toward Geomoru village.

Every house is engraved with hundred-pacer viper

totems. Some verdant hills are served as back door screens.

Within hundred paces there are everywhere millet, roselle,

red quinoa, coffee, custard apple, not just for good looking,

I taste here all those sweet varieties never before.

Along the half-dried streaming Kanadun Creek,

the villagers have bathed under the sunshine

in busy agricultural production works.

The tour buses are idle for waiting

those bathed in hot springs.

2020.07.19

Climbing up the Hilltop in Keelung

Along Rongxuan Trail in Keelung
I walk along the stone steps in early morning,
expecting to find better scenery at higher level.
Among the dense leaves of the big banyan,
a number of fibrous roots growing down to ground,
the birds begin to sing chorus in symphony.
The weeds and wildflowers beckon me along the
        path.
I look up and find the white clouds in smiling,
to inspire me the poetic feeling in my mind
after the baptism with many winds and rains.
The stone steps in meandering
lead me going up and up all the way
until the viewing platform on the hilltop.
Overlooking the vast magnificent ocean
which displays the strong spirit of surfing waves,

the turbulent currents against the distant challenges,
I stand independently in silence at the hilltop,
feel wholeheartedly my homeland of Taiwan island
staying alone between heaven and earth proudly.

2020.09.30

The Luce Chapel

In early morning
the clock
is still in peaceful sleeping.
There is melodious voice
leading me to here.
I look back in front of the clock tower
watching you to put both hands together
praying toward the sky.
Among the clouds,
it reveals a trace of morning sun
shining on
your fingertips.
I want to lie on the surrounding
green good earth
as my eternal bed.

2020.11.15

Centennial Elegance and Happiness

Your daughter Ying-ying

takes along your legacy memento, a lavender jade,

hanging in front of my chest,

your image immediately

appears on my heart.

On the front side of the jade

it was carved with "carp jumping over the dragon
>> gate"

while I have been guarding the cage gate of poetry.

On the back side of the jade,

it was carved with "flowers blooming rich and noble"

while I have been chasing for the restoration of
>> beauty.

In commemoration of the centennial anniversary of
poetess Chen Hsiu-si, this jade becomes
a sign that I am blessed with
the elegance and happiness.

2020.11.17

Green Tunnel at Sicao

Long long ago passing through the black tunnel
the space was filled with coal dusts.
Among the dark around
suddenly a strong ray of white light
would make everyone spirit dispersed.
Now passing through the green tunnel,
the bamboo raft slides slowly
over the emerald green river course
surrounded by abundant mangroves.
Sunlight casts through the leaf gaps
reflecting another world in the water.
The fiddler crabs raise their claws as flags
reflective in the dream.

2021.03.24

Isolation

I isolate myself from society
staying alone in my study
because COVID-19 pandemic.

The birds isolate from their cages
returning to the forest
flying freely among the trees.

The soul isolates from the body
proceeding international poetry communication
without any hindrance.

Our territory
isolates from evil neighbor
becoming an entity of independence.

2021.06.08

Tamsui Arts & Cultural Park

Long long ago I heard
gasp sounds of driving light train,
smooth sounds of the pump pumping kerosene,
mechanical sounds of beating tin plates to make cans,
splashing sounds of seaplane taking off and landing
        on the river,
panic sounds of the U.S. plane bombing to burn out
        the oil storage.

Then it becomes
sounds of bricks and roof tiles moaning in the rain,
sounds of small grasses joyful laughing under the
        sunshine,
sounds of cicadas in summer calling for life,
sounds of butterflies lightly flapping their wings to
        beckon the bees,

sounds of big tree lonely resisting the suppressed
winds.

Now, I often hear
wisdom sounds of discussions in the classroom of
Community College,
tender sounds of poetry recitals at the new book
release,
passionate sounds of young musicians on the concert,
inner sounds of appreciation from the visitors to the
art exhibition,
pleasant sounds of visitors in feeling nostalgic and
exploring new found.

2021.08.13

Cudweed Herbal Rice Cakes

A group of poets

came to Stone Wall House at Tiong-liâu Village,

with their hands used to write poetry

together making cudweed herbal rice cakes.

After steaming,

either the red bean cakes

or the dried radish cakes,

or taro cakes,

every piece of the stuffings

all became poetry.

2021.09.20

Bronze Statue Smile

The bronze statue causes controversy
whether it might entitle to occupy such high position?
No matter some people go to protest in groups,
and shout fierce slogans on the square,
the bronze statue smile forever reveals
unreal nature.
That is the serious cold sneer
molded after casting and cooling.
He slaughtered people during his lifetime,
satisfied with making praises by his followers.
No matter how is the controversy
he will be remained in history
sneered by people.

2020.10.03

Longing for Tiong-liâu

The landscape of Tiong-liâu has been blessed by God.

The field land in Tiong-liâu was cultivated by our
ancestors.

The culture of Tiong-liâu has been established by
generations.

I lived in Tiong-liâu when I was young.

I departed from Tiong-liâu since I entered into middle
age.

I do my best to repay for Tiong-liâu in my later stage.

After baptized by poetry all my life,

I have been frequently longing for Tiong-liâu,

the last base of love,

as my eternal resting place.

2021.10.05

Tamsui Concert

On the riverside of Tamsui,

among the flowing melodies of the music composed

from the outstanding poems by Dr. Tu Tsung-ming,

I intoxicated myself into the autumn wind,

as if the fluttering Tamsui eagle

drifts in the sky

in front of the huge rock wall at Baraka hill*.

Ah, my teenager dream

has been still wandered

among the repeated calls of autumn wind,

never woken up yet.

∗ The native home of Dr. Tu Tsung-ming was located in a deep village
 among the forest on Baraka hill. There is a huge rock wall on the
 hill that can be seen from Tiong-liâu village afar.

2021.10.16

Sunflower in Ukraine

I put the seeds of sunflower
into the pocket of my military uniform,
ready to change my flesh body at the battlefield
as the culture medium of soils
and to irrigate them with my blood
on the sovereign territory in Ukraine.

I keep in mind the advice of my bride
to bear witness with by new uniform on site,
when demobilization after war to cultivate
and to protect this species of national flower
smiling toward the sky
on my free homeland in Ukraine.

2022.02.27

Fallen Leaves

The yellow leaves
fell from whole row of
Madagascar Almond
all over the ground just one night.
The television
broadcasts suddenly
the missile bombings
in the distance.
All lives are like the yellow leaves
messy lying on the ground,
then swept into the trench
hastily buried.

2022.03.08

My Books

My books are
my nostalgia to hometown
in all my life.

My books are
the nutrition injected from my friends
to be accumulated in my body.

My books are
the foreign ideas crossing the ocean
to live with me together.

My books are
the loves that Taiwan gave me layers upon layers
inseparable.

My books are
at last residing forever in my hometown
in Tamsui.

2022.07.26

River View

One drop water, two drops water, three drops
    water......
flow into the beside creek
that rehabilitated as an aquatic animals leisure park,
then gather to become a stream
passing through a long journey
to reach the peaceful Tamsui River
by the way pushing the sunset to the estuary.
The echo of history has disappeared
yet seems still be heard in the dark.
The blessing lamps are lighted at the foot of Mount
    Guanyin.
A small boat is rowing slowly across the river
as if to draw a zipper
let the river close its eyes for rest.

2022.09.18

Sky Hall

At higher place I can look far distance
even look down the long river of history
and joyful human life.
I look around by extreme sight
just like a hero rebirth
to talk about the old story of Tamsui.
Until ultimate satisfactory,
the darkness falls,
lights on,
I am gong to shift to another battlefield
preparing for next struggle.

2022.09.18

On Dreamland of Golden Tulip

The sun rises from the east.
On the peak of Mount Guanyin
only a few strands of white cloud hairs remain.
The birds get up earlier than me,
flying go and fro
in front of the window to watch me.
The human world is so quiet
that I prefer to stay in my dreamland
laying in the arms of golden tulip,
not to wake up.

2022.09.18

Tiong-liâu Poetry Road

All roads lead to the home,

every day we go out walking on the way home.

In my eternal hometown, may I ask

where does the Tiong-liâu poetry road lead to?

It is along the whispers of ditch water

accompanied by the chirping of birds,

mixed with the rustles of bamboo leaves in the wind.

Occasionally, there is also joyful sound

that the big leave palm of giant taro

catching the raindrops fallen accidentally.

You may listen the poems whispering to you

while walk step by step to the home of the soul

on Tiong-liâu poetry road.

2022.09.19

The Statues of Egrets

At foothills of Datun Mountain,
the egrets patrol the irrigating water.
In addition, also buffalos and rice fields.
compose as a rural farming picture.
This is my childhood memory,
serene and harmonious.
Seventy years have passed,
the farmland has been transformed
into an active ecological community.
The egrets have migrated to new position
fixed standing under the Osmanthus tree
to guide the direction of poetry road.

2022.09.22

Making Pottery

Come!
Please use your gentle hands
patting me, rubbing me, rolling me,
and pressing me into a flat body
which still insists the essence on enough resistance,
molding me into a fixed form,
pinching me into an available utensil,
further decorating me with warm plain color
moreover, painting a morning star
forever guiding me
the forward direction to independence.

2022.10.04

Imagination

On the curved surface roof

paved as wavy lawn slip slope,

there are planted with two groups of tulips.

One group is integrated as a sweet potato island

         contour,

another group is surrounded to become a heart shape.

Everyday the golden sun

like the Magi from the east

comes daily on pilgrimage

and does not forget

confessing to the dewdrops:

I love Taiwan!

2022.10.08

Descending to the Human World

I dreamt of a female painter
dressed with black thin waist and wide swing,
appearing in front of the lofty church on the hill.
Her figure was more elegant than the zigzag ladder,
the yellow flower in her bun
was more vivid than the flowers on the street trees.
Buenos días, señor!
Buenos días, señorita!
Beauty and poetry competed to each other in silence,
the creation was finished in the sacred moment
to bring the soul from a higher step
descending to the human world.
At the instant when I was dazed
the cock crowed!

2022.12.05

In Memory
of First Snow in Early Year at Tamsui

The snow falling constantly
thinks continuously about
the love unforgettable from the previous life
until the fate that cannot be denied in this life.
When the snow falls constantly
the world is empty without anything,
that kind of cold
turns into the spontaneous warmth in my heart
and leave behind the unlimited nostalgia.
The snow is really unforgettable.

2023.08.28

Book Donation
——To Chueh-sheng Memorial Library of Tamkang University

The book collection in my study
is my belief in lifetime unceasingly,
accumulates my dreams known no whereabouts
as well as unwavering commitment,
finally handed over to the Library of Tamkang
                University in my hometown
located over one hilltop of Five-Tiger Hills
in spreading the fragrance from history that lasts
                forever.
It might meets someone in sometime
smelling the secrets in the book collection,
at the moment of consonance
the seed falls
naturally looking up at the sunrise of Datun Mountain,
breeding the nostalgia of Taiwan.

2022.09.02

The Peace Park

I look out over the sea at Tamsui
extending the view to Taiwan Strait
under broad ocean and vast sky to communicate
    outside world.
I look up at Guanyin Mountain
while calm down my mind and cultivate my character
to reach far far away until the paradise world.
In the peace park
along the Ho-be Art and Poetry Trail,
the landscape presented by poetry and painting
    creations
is co-existence with great nature.
There is a virtual Bodhi tree
erected forever in my deep heart.

2023.09.17

My Verses

My verses

are the words of freedom and loneliness

by free and natural arrangement,

but enter by mistake into the book forest in the
  library,

confused as the result of lost direction

freely remaining in the silent space

to become a lonely poem

alone just like

my figure in the dusk.

2023.09.22

Poetry Cultivates Our Life
—— To poet Lee Chang-hsien

In your romantic youth years

you started to write poems caring about reality.

When you worked as the manager at the electronics
    factory

what you always think about is the life of female
    workers.

Going abroad in middle age to promote international
    cooperation,

you never forgot the security of Taiwan.

At the age you retired from work position,

you experienced enough enjoy the tea with fragrant
    out of bitter.

In your leisure time after successful poetry writing,

you devoted yourself to calligraphy, engraving and
    making pottery.

Now, I find you are endeavoring to art creation,

burning verses onto teacups,

let's drink up the poetic emotion,

and the beauty of poetry will be remained in the
world forever.

2023.09.24

The Songs come from Kenya

The songs come from Kenya,
musician Ombiro sings his passionate songs
in consonance with his own made eight-string
        cowhide drum
almost to take away the minds of audiences.
From the concert hall of University on hill top
to the Sky Hall of Golden Tulip Hotel,
to Tiong-liâu Community,
to the Shell Restaurant overlooking Tamsui River,
the lingering sounds of his songs are unceasing,
at last the improvisation he composes for me
makes my soul intoxicated
with all fingers fly dancing.

＊Kenyan musician Wilfred Ombiro came to Tamsui in accompany with Kenyan poet Christopher Okemwa to participate 2023 Formosa International Poetry Festival. His performance was wholeheartedly welcome. At closing banquet, I was honored by his music composed for me.

2023.09.30

Poisonous Scorpions

The poisonous scorpions raise their long claws,
as soon as seeing the flowers smiling in the wind,
just tear their petals apart and destroy them all over,
as soon as encountering the hard-working ants
just massacres the innocent objects all out.
What fallen one after another from the sky in Middle
        East
are not the sympathetic tears
but more vicious rocket missiles,
the flames and black smokes arise therewith
cannot blind the human minds.

✱ On October 7, 2023, the Palestinian militant organization Hamas
launched thousands of rocket missiles to sneaky attack on Israel,
triggering a fierce Israeli-Hamas war.

2023.10.13

As a "Li" Poetry Farmer for 60 Years

As soon as meeting you,
I have decided to serve as a farmer all my life,
wearing with a bamboo hat
endeavoring to cultivate poetry fields.
I run among the urban high buildings like jungles
to seek for the nutritious matter of life being,
dig deep in the mines of words
to sift through treasures left behind by predecessors,
wander around the mysterious mountains of thought
to explore and discover the new territories.
I have insisted this farming for 60 years
and become haggard little by little
looked like a withered tree.

2023.10.15

A Love Poem to Tainan

Hard work in bud for four hundred years
to look forward having a bright blooming smile
attracting everyone to appreciate together
the moonlight peeking out from the cloud layers.

2023.11.24

著者簡介 *About Poet*

　　李魁賢，曾任國家文化藝術基金會董事長、國立中正大學台灣文學研究所兼任教授，台南和淡水福爾摩莎國際詩歌節策畫，現任世界詩人運動組織（Movimiento Poetas del Mundo）副會長（2014～）。

　　詩被翻譯在日本、韓國、加拿大、紐西蘭、荷蘭、南斯拉夫、羅馬尼亞、印度、希臘、立陶宛、美國、西班牙、巴西、蒙古、俄羅斯、古巴、智利、波蘭、尼加拉瓜、孟加拉、土耳其、馬其頓、塞爾維亞、馬來西亞、科索沃、義大利、墨西哥、哥倫比亞、阿拉伯聯合大公國、尼泊爾、肯亞、阿爾巴尼亞、南非共和國、英國等國發表。

應邀參加過韓國、日本、印度、蒙古、薩爾瓦多、尼加拉瓜、古巴、智利、緬甸、孟加拉、馬其頓、秘魯、突尼西亞、羅馬尼亞、墨西哥等國之國際詩歌節。

獲吳濁流文學獎新詩獎、巫永福評論獎、韓國亞洲詩人貢獻獎、榮後台灣詩獎、賴和文學獎、行政院文化獎、印度麥氏學會（Michael Madhusudan Academy）詩人獎、台灣新文學貢獻獎、吳三連獎新詩獎、蒙古建國八百週年成吉思汗金牌、真理大學台灣文學家牛津獎、孟加拉卡塔克文學獎（Kathak Literary Award）、馬其頓奈姆・弗拉舍里（Naim Frashëri）文學獎、秘魯特里爾塞金獎和金幟獎、台灣國家文藝獎、印度首席傑出詩獎、蒙特內哥羅（黑

山）共和國文學翻譯協會文學翻譯獎、塞爾維亞「神草」（Raskovnik）文學藝術協會國際卓越詩藝一級騎士獎、美國李察・安吉禮紀念舞詩競賽第三獎等。

Lee Kuei-shien(b. 1937), served as chairman of National Culture and Arts Foundation in Taiwan from 2005 to 2007, the organizer of Formosa International poetry Festival from 2016 to 2021, now is the vice president in Asia of Movimiento Poetas del Mundo since 2014.

He published 29 poetry books and 3 memoires. His poems have been translated and published in Japan, Korea, Canada, New Zealand, Netherlands, Yugoslavia, Romania, India, Greece, Lithuania, USA, Spain, Brazil, Mongolia, Russia, Cuba, Chile, Poland, Nicaragua, Bangladesh, Turkey, Macedonia, Serbia, Malaysia, Kosovo, Italy, Mexico, Colombia, The United Arab Emirates, Nepal, Kenya, Albania, South Africa, England, etc.

He was invited to participate the international poetry festival held in Korea, Japan, India, Mongolia, El Salvador, Nicaragua, Cuba, Chile, Myanmar, Bangladesh,

Macedonia, Peru, Tunisia, Romania, Mexico, etc.

He was awarded with Wu Cho-liu Award of New Poetry(1975), Wu Yong-fu Award of Literature Criticism(1986), Merit of Asian Poet, Korea(1994), Ronghou Taiwanese Poet Prize, Taiwan(1997), World Poet of the Year 1997, Poets International, India(1998), Poet of the Millennium Award, International poets Academy, India(2000), Lai Ho Literature Prize and Premier Culture Prize, both in Taiwan(2001). He also received the Michael Madhusudan Poet Award from Michael Madhusudan Academy(2002), Wu San-lien Prize in Literature(2004), Poet Medal from Mongolian Cultural Foundation(2005), Chinggis Khaan Golden Medal for 800 Anniversary of Mongolian State(2006), Oxford Award for Taiwan Writers(2011), Award of CKorean Literature of Korea(2013), Kathak Literary Award of Bangladesh(2016),

Literary Prize "Naim Frashëri" of Macedonia(2016), "Trilce de Oro" of Peru(2017), National Culture and Arts Prize of Taiwan(2018), Bandera Iluminada of Peru(2018), Prime Poetry Award for Excellence of India(2019), and Literary Award for Translation from Association of Literary Translators of Montenegro(Udruzenje knjizevnih prevodilaca Crne Gore)(2020), International Award "A Knight of the First Order of Noble Skills in Poetry" from "Raskovnik" Literary and Artistic Association, Smederevo, Serbia(2020), Third Prize in the Richard Angilly Memorial Dancing Poetry Contest, USA(2023).

語言文學類　PG3030　名流詩叢51

太陽之子
──李魁賢台華英三語詩集
The Son of Sun

作　　者／李魁賢（Lee Kuei-shien）
責任編輯／吳霽恆
圖文排版／許絜瑀
封面設計／張家碩

發　行　人／宋政坤
法律顧問／毛國樑　律師
出版發行／秀威資訊科技股份有限公司
　　　　　114台北市內湖區瑞光路76巷65號1樓
　　　　　電話：+886-2-2796-3638　傳真：+886-2-2796-1377
　　　　　http://www.showwe.com.tw
劃撥帳號／19563868　戶名：秀威資訊科技股份有限公司
　　　　　讀者服務信箱：service@showwe.com.tw
展售門市／國家書店（松江門市）
　　　　　104台北市中山區松江路209號1樓
　　　　　電話：+886-2-2518-0207　傳真：+886-2-2518-0778
網路訂購／秀威網路書店：https://store.showwe.tw
　　　　　國家網路書店：https://www.govbooks.com.tw

2024年3月　BOD一版
定價：220元
版權所有　翻印必究
本書如有缺頁、破損或裝訂錯誤，請寄回更換

讀者回函卡

國家圖書館出版品預行編目

太陽之子:李魁賢台華英三語詩集 = The son of sun / 李
魁賢著. -- 一版. -- 臺北市:秀威資訊科技股份有限公司,
2024.03
　　面;　公分. -- (語言文學類;PG3030)(名流詩叢;51)
部分內容為英文
BOD版
ISBN 978-626-7346-66-2(平裝)

863.51   113001173